A loud whinny split the air. Jack saw a beautiful horse rearing up.

She had no rider or saddle, just a rope around her neck. She was as red as the sunset. She had a wild black mane and a white star above her eyes.

"We can't keep fighting this one, boss!" a cowboy yelled.

"Yes. She wants her foal," another said. "We shouldn't have left him behind."

"He was too slow," a growly voice said. "We'll sell her when we cross the border."

That's terrible! thought Jack. He knew Annie must be upset too.

Read all the adventures of
Jack and **Annie**!

1–4: The Mystery of the Tree House

5–8: The Mystery of the Magic Spell

9–12: The Mystery of the Ancient Riddles

Coming soon:

Magic Tree House™

A WILD WEST RIDE

MARY POPE OSBORNE

Illustrated by Philippe Masson

RED FOX

A WILD WEST RIDE

A RED FOX BOOK 978 1 862 30571 7

Published in Great Britain by Red Fox,
an imprint of Random House Children's Books
A Random House Group Company

Published in the US as *Ghost Town at Sundown* by Random House Children's
Books, a division of Random House Inc, 1997

Red Fox edition published 2009

1 3 5 7 9 10 8 6 4 2

The Random House Group Limited supports the Forest Stewardship
Council (FSC), the leading international forest certification organization.
All our titles that are printed on Greenpeace-approved FSC-certified paper carry
the FSC logo. Our paper procurement policy can be found at
www.rbooks.co.uk/environment.

Set in 16/21pt Bembo MT Schoolbook by
Falcon Oast Graphic Art Ltd.

Red Fox Books are published by Random House Children's Books,
61–63 Uxbridge Road, London W5 5SA

www.**kids**at**randomhouse**.com
www.**rbooks**.co.uk

Addresses for companies within The Random House Group Limited can be found
at: www.randomhouse.co.uk/offices.htm

THE RANDOM HOUSE GROUP Limited Reg. No. 954009

A CIP catalogue record for this book is available from the British Library.

Printed in the UK by CPI Bookmarque, Croydon, CR0 4TD

For Nick Plakias — wonderful friend and singing cowboy poet

Dear Reader,

Over the past year, many of you have asked me to send Jack and Annie to the Wild West. I thought this was a good idea, but I wasn't sure what should happen in the story.

Then one day, I received a letter from a girl named Alexandra, who lives in Washington, US. She suggested that Jack and Annie help a foal to find his mother, who has been stolen by horse thieves.

What an excellent idea, I thought. Many thanks to Alexandra for helping me with this book.

Also, thanks to everyone who has written. More Magic Tree House books are in the planning . . . so all your thoughts and suggestions are very welcome. Keep them coming!

Mary Pope Osborne

Contents

1

How Wild?

Jack and Annie were sitting on the veranda of their house. Annie was gazing down the street at the Frog Valley woods. Jack was reading a book.

"I have a feeling we should check the woods again," said Annie.

"Why?" said Jack, without looking up.

"A rabbit's hopping by," said Annie.

"So? We've seen rabbits before."

"Not like this one," said Annie.

"What do you mean?" Jack stood up and looked with her.

He saw a rabbit with very long legs hopping down their street. Soon the rabbit left the pavement and headed into the woods.

"He's a sign," said Annie.

"A sign of *what*?" asked Jack.

"That Morgan's back," said Annie. She jumped off the veranda. 'Come on!'

"But what about dinner?" Jack said. "Dad told us it would be ready soon."

"Don't worry," said Annie. "You know that when we leave in the tree house, time stops."

She ran across their front garden.

Jack pulled on his rucksack. "Back in ten minutes!" he called through the doorway. Then he followed Annie.

They hurried down the street and into
the Frog Valley woods. The sun was
setting above the trees.

"There he is!" said Annie.

The rabbit was standing in a ray of sunlight. When he saw them, he ran off again.

Jack and Annie followed the rabbit until he vanished behind the tallest tree.

"I told you! See?" said Annie, panting. She pointed up at the tree.

Morgan le Fay was waving to them from the magic tree house, high in the branches.

Jack and Annie waved back to her. As always, Jack was very happy to see the enchantress librarian again.

"Come up!" she called.

Annie and Jack started up the rope ladder. They climbed up to the tree house.

"We followed a strange rabbit here," said Annie. 'Is he your friend?'

"Perhaps," said Morgan. She smiled mysteriously. "I have many odd friends."

"Including us," said Annie.

Morgan laughed. "That's right."

"How are you?" said Jack.

"I'm still having problems with Merlin," said the enchantress, "which leaves me little time to do my real work. But soon you will both become Master Librarians, and that will be a big help to me."

Jack smiled. He was going to be a Master Librarian who travelled through time and space. It was almost too good to believe.

"Are you ready to solve another riddle?" asked Morgan.

"Yes!" said Jack and Annie together.

"Good," said Morgan. "First, you'll need this for research . . ."

She pulled a book from her robe and handed it to Jack. It was the book that would help them on their journey.

The title of the book was *Days of the Wild West*. On the cover was a picture of a town from the Old West on a prairie.

"Oh, wow," said Annie. "The Wild West!"

Jack took a deep breath. *Just how wild?* he wondered.

Morgan reached into the folds of her robe again and pulled out a scroll. She handed it to Annie.

"Read this when the tree house lands," she said.

"Is it the riddle?" asked Jack.

"Yes," said Morgan. "Then you'll only have two more to solve. Are you ready to go?"

Jack and Annie nodded. Annie pointed to the picture on the cover of the Wild West book.

"I wish we could go there," she said.

The wind started to blow.

"Goodbye!" said Morgan. "Good luck!"

The tree house started to spin.

Jack squeezed his eyes shut.

The tree house spun faster and faster.

Then everything was still.

Absolutely still.

Jack opened his eyes.

Morgan le Fay was gone.

A fly buzzed around his head.

2

Rattlesnake Flats

The air was hot and dry.

Jack and Annie peeped outside.

The tree house had landed in a lone tree on a prairie. The sun was low in the sky.

Right in front of them was the town from the cover of the book. In real life it looked empty and spooky.

To one side of the town was a patch of ground with several gravestones.

"That's creepy," said Annie.

"I know," said Jack. He took a deep breath. "What does our riddle say?"

Annie held up the ancient scroll. She
unrolled it. Then she and Jack read
together:

> "*Out of the blue,*
> *my lonely voice*
> *calls out to you.*
> *Who am I? Am I?*"

Jack pushed his glasses into place and
read the riddle again to himself.

"There must be a mistake," he said. "*Am I?* is written twice."

"Well, I don't hear *any* voices now," Annie said as she looked out of the window.

There was no human sounds at all – only the buzzing of flies and the whistling of the dry wind.

"Let's look at the book," Jack said.

He opened the book. The pages were yellow with age. He found a picture of the town and read the words beneath it out loud:

"*In the 1870s, Rattlesnake Flats was a rest stop for the stagecoach that carried passengers from Santa Fe, New Mexico, to Fort Worth, Texas. When the river dried up, everyone left. By 1880, it was a ghost town.*"

"Wow, a *ghost* town," said Annie, her eyes wide.

"Let's take a quick look round," said Jack. "So we can leave before dark."

"OK," said Annie. "Let's hurry." She started down the rope ladder.

Jack put the old book into his bag. Then he followed Annie down the ladder.

They stood by the tree and looked about. Bundles of dry grass blew across the ground.

Suddenly something jumped past them.

"What was that?" they both said.

It was just a rabbit – a lone, long-legged rabbit hopping past them.

"He's just like that rabbit we saw at home," said Jack.

"Yes, that rabbit must have been a sign of things to come," said Annie.

The rabbit hopped away and out of sight.

"I'd better take notes," said Jack.

He reached into his rucksack and took out his notebook and pencil.

He wrote:

rabbits with long legs

"What's that sound?" said Annie.

"What sound?" asked Jack.

"That rattling sound!" said Annie.

Jack looked up. "*What?*" he said.

"There!" Annie pointed to a rattlesnake. It was about thirty metres away. It was coiled up and rattling.

Jack took one look at the snake and ran. Annie ran too. They ran past the graveyard and into the ghost town."

"I guess that's why this town is called

Rattlesnake Flats," said Annie when they
stopped.

Jack looked around. The place was
hardly big enough to call a town. There
was one unpaved street and a few old
buildings.

It was quiet — too quiet.

"Look, a shop," said Annie.

She pointed to a building. The faded
sign said GENERAL STORE. "Let's look
inside. Maybe the answer to the riddle is
in there."

Jack and Annie stepped onto the veranda. The wooden boards creaked loudly. The door had fallen off its hinges. They peeped inside.

The air was thick with dust. Cobwebs hung from the ceiling.

"Maybe we shouldn't go in," said Jack.

"But what if the answer's there?" said Annie. "Let's just have a quick look."

Jack took a deep breath. "OK."

He and Annie tiptoed into the shop.

"Look," said Annie. She picked up a pair of rusty spurs.

"Careful," said Jack. He poked at other stuff in the shop – an old feed sack, a rusty tin mug, a faded calendar dated 1878.

"Oh, wow," said Annie. She held up two cowboy hats. She put one on and handed the other one to Jack. "For you."

"It's too dusty," said Jack.

"Just blow on it," said Annie.

Jack blew on his hat. A cloud of dust rose up. He sneezed.

"Just try it on!" said Annie.

Jack put the hat on. It nearly covered his eyes.

"Boots!" said Annie. She pointed to a row of cowboy boots on a shelf. "There are even some small ones our size. Here's a pair for you." She handed the boots to Jack.

"They're not ours," he said.

"I know, but just try them on," said Annie.

Jack turned his boots upside down and shook them as hard as he could.

"What are you doing?" Annie asked, pulling on another pair of boots.

"Checking for scorpions," Jack said.

"Ja-ack." Annie laughed. "Try them on!"

Jack sighed. He pulled off his shoes and pushed his feet into the boots. He pushed and pushed. The boots were really stiff.

Finally he got his feet inside. Then he tried to walk.

"Owww!" he said. "Forget it." He started to pull off the boots.

"What's that?" Annie said.

Jack froze.

"Piano music," said Annie. "Maybe the person playing it is the voice in the riddle! Come on!"

Jack threw his trainers into his rucksack and hobbled after Annie.

3

Player Piano

Outside, the sad tune played on.

"It's coming from over there," said Annie.

She crept towards a building that had a sign with the word HOTEL on it. Jack limped after her.

Annie slowly pushed open a swing door. They peeped inside.

The fading daylight lit a piano in the corner of the room. The keys were moving up and down. But no one was there!

"Wow!" whispered Annie. "A ghost playing the piano!"

Suddenly the keys were still. The air got very cold.

"No. No way," said Jack. "There's no such thing as a ghost."

"We saw one in ancient Egypt," whispered Annie.

"Yes, but that was ancient Egypt," said Jack. Even so, his heart raced.

"I'll look it up." Jack pulled out the Wild West book. He found a picture of a piano. He read aloud:

"Player pianos were popular in America's Old West. The piano played automatically when someone pumped its floor pedals. Later, with the help of electricity, the piano played all by itself."

"Phew." Jack closed the book. "I knew there was an answer," he said. "It must be electric, and somehow it came on."

"I didn't know they had electricity in the Wild West," said Annie.

"They didn't," said Jack.

He looked at Annie. "Oh, no, let's get out of here!" he said.

Jack and Annie backed out of the hotel.

When they got outside, they heard another sound – horses' hooves thumping against the hard ground.

A cloud of dust seemed to be moving towards the town. As it got closer, Jack saw three riders. They were herding a small group of horses.

"Hide!" Jack said.

"Where?" said Annie.

Jack looked around wildly. He saw two barrels outside the hotel.

"There!" he said.

Jack and Annie hurried over to the empty barrels. Jack climbed inside one and tried to scrunch down. His hat wouldn't fit! He jumped out of the barrel and threw his hat into the hotel.

"Mine too!" said Annie.

Jack grabbed hers and threw it too.
Then he scrambled back into the barrel.
Just in time.

Jack heard the horses thunder into
town. He peeped through a crack in the
barrel and saw a blur of cowboys and
horses go by.

"*Whoa! Whoa! Whoa!*" men shouted.

Jack heard the horses come to a halt.
They stamped and snorted, but through
the crack, all he could see was shadows.

Dust covered Jack. He needed to
sneeze. He pinched his nose.

"The river bed must have dried up!" a
cowboy yelled. "This town's a ghost!"

"Yes, it gives me the shivers," said
another. "Let's camp over that hill."

Jack *really* needed to sneeze now. He

pinched his nose tighter. But he couldn't stop the sneeze. He let out a choked "*A-tchoo!*"

"What was that?" someone said.

Just then a loud whinny split the air. Jack saw a beautiful horse rearing up.

She had no rider or saddle, just a rope around her neck. She was as red as the sunset. She had a wild black mane and a white star above her eyes.

"We can't keep fighting this one, boss!" a cowboy yelled.

"Yes. She wants her foal," another said. "We shouldn't have left him behind."

"He was too slow," a growly voice said. "We'll sell her when we cross the border."

That's terrible! thought Jack. He knew

Annie must be upset too. He just hoped she wouldn't jump out of her barrel.

But the cowboys pulled the red horse away. The ground rang from the pounding of hooves as they galloped off.

Jack and Annie stood up. They watched the riders disappear into the dust. The pounding faded away. All was quiet again, except for the lazy buzzing of flies.

"They were cruel to that horse," Annie said in a low, angry voice.

"I know. But there was nothing we could do," said Jack. His boots were killing him. He climbed out of his barrel.

"Ow! I have to get these off," he said.

Jack sat down on the veranda of the hotel. He grabbed the foot of one boot and pulled.

"Jack," said Annie, "I think there is something we can do."

"What?" Jack looked up.

A little horse was galloping down the road. He was as red as the wild mother horse. He had the same black mane and white star above his eyes.

A rope was around his neck. He looked very lost.

4

Hands Up!

"It's the foal!" said Annie. "He's looking for his mother!"

She ran towards the wild-eyed little horse.

"Wait!" called Jack. "Oh, no." He pulled the book out of his bag.

He found a chapter called "Horses of the Wild West". He started reading.

"*At the end of the 1800s, over a million wild horses, called mustangs, wandered the West. These tough, fast horses were descendants of runaway Spanish horses. Mustang herders captured them and sold them to ranchers. Breaking a wild mustang took great skill.*"

Jack turned the page. There was a picture of a herd of horses. Two of them even looked like the beautiful mare and her foal.

"Annie!" Jack called. "You should see this picture."

Annie didn't answer.

Jack looked up.

Annie was trying to get close to the young mustang, but he kept darting away.

"Be careful! He's wild!" said Jack.

Annie was speaking softly to the young horse.

She slowly reached out and grabbed the end of his rope. Still talking to him, she led him over to a broad wooden post.

"Stop! Don't do anything!" said Jack.

He flicked through the pages of his book. He found a section called "How to Treat a Horse".

The basic rules on how to treat a horse are simple: a soft hand, a firm voice, a sunny attitude, praise and reward.

"I've got the rules!" shouted Jack. "Don't do anything until I've written them down!"

Jack pulled out his notebook and pencil. He wrote:

Horse Rules
1. soft hand
2. firm voice
3. sunny attitude
4. praise
5. reward

"OK, listen." Jack looked up.
But Annie was already sitting on

the young horse's back!

Jack froze. He held his breath.

The mustang whinnied and pawed the ground. He snorted and tossed his head.

Annie kept patting his neck and talking softly.

Finally he grew still.

Annie smiled at Jack. "I've named him Sunset," she said.

Jack let out his breath.

"Let's go," said Annie climbing down. "We have to take him to his mum."

"Are you crazy?" said Jack. "We have to solve our riddle. It'll be dark soon. And those cowboys were nasty, I could tell."

"We don't have any choice," said Annie.

"Oh, no." Jack knew she wouldn't change her mind. "Let's see what the book says." He read more about mustangs:

"Wild mustangs live together in families. The bond between a mare and her foal is very strong. His sounds of distress or hunger will always bring her to him. A mustang cannot bear to wander alone."

Jack groaned. He looked at Sunset. The young mustang did have a sad look in his eyes.

"OK, we'll make a plan," he said. "But first I have to get these boots off."

Jack grabbed one of his boots and pulled.

"Hurry!" said Annie.

"I can't even think in these things!" said Jack.

He huffed and puffed and pulled. Then a deep voice stopped him cold: "Hands up – or I'll shoot!"

33

Jack let go of his boot. He raised his hands in the air. So did Annie.

A cowboy rode out of an alley. His face was bony and tanned. He was riding a grey horse and pointing a gun at them.

"I reckon you're the smallest horse thieves I've ever come across," he said.

5

Slim

"We're not horse thieves!" said Annie.

"Well then, what are you doing with my horse here?" he said.

"Some cowboys came through town with his mother," said Annie. "They left him behind because he was too slow."

"Yup, must be the horse thieves that stole my last five mustangs," the cowboy said.

"Who are you?" said Jack.

"I'm a mustang herder," the cowboy said.

"They rode through town. Then Sunset arrived all alone," said Annie. "We're taking him to his mother."

"Sunset?" the cowboy said.

"Yes." Annie smiled. "I named him."

The cowboy put away his gun.

"Well, you're pretty brave to try and rescue him, Smiley," he said.

"Thanks," said Annie.

Jack cleared his throat. "A mustang needs his family," he said. "The bond between a mare and her foal is very strong."

The cowboy looked at Jack. "Whoa, you're pretty smart to know that, Shorty."

"Shorty?" said Jack.

"Every cowboy's got to have a nickname," said the cowboy.

"What's yours?" said Annie.

"Slim," said the cowboy. "My name is

Slim Cooley. And
this is Dusty." He
patted his horse.

"That suits you,"
said Annie.

Jack agreed. Slim
was slim. And Dusty
was dusty.

"So tell me," Slim
said. "How did you
two brave young'uns
end up in Rattlesnake
Flats?"

Jack caught his breath.
He didn't know how to
explain it.

"Um . . . the stagecoach," said
Annie. "We begged the driver to let
us off. But I think we made a mistake."

Slim looked around. "I'll say," he said.

"When the next one comes through,
we're leaving," said Annie.

"I see," said Slim. "Well, I'm going to take my mustang now and find those thieves. You didn't hear where they were headed, did you?"

"They said they were going to camp over that hill," said Jack.

"Hmm, must be over there," said Slim. He looked at a low hill in the distance. The sun was a red ball above it.

"Better get going before dark," he said.

"Can we come with you?" said Annie.

"No, we have to stay here," Jack said quickly. Now that Slim could help Sunset, Jack wanted to look for the answer to the riddle. Plus, he still wanted to take off his boots.

"Shorty's right to be scared," Slim said to Annie. "This is no job for young'uns."

"Scared?" said Jack.

"Oh, please! I want to go," said Annie.

Slim looked at Jack. "And what do you want, Shorty?"

For starters, he wanted Slim to stop calling him Shorty. And he wanted Slim to think he was brave.

"Yes, I want to go too," said Jack.

"What about your stagecoach?" asked Slim.

"It's not coming until tomorrow," Annie said quickly.

"Well . . ." Slim scratched his chin. "I reckon I could use some good help. But you have to do everything I say."

"We will!" said Annie. "Can I ride Sunset?"

"I wouldn't say yes to many kids, Smiley, but you seem to have a knack with horses," said Slim. "Now, hang on tight to his mane – I'll just pull him along behind me."

Slim slipped the rope off the post. Then he held his hand out to Jack.

"Put your foot in the stirrup, Shorty. And grab my hand," said Slim.

Jack did as Slim said. Slim pulled him onto the front of his saddle.

Jack held onto the pommel of the saddle.

"Sit tight," said Slim. "It's not far."

Slim shook his reins. Dusty set off with Sunset right behind him.

Jack bounced up and down. His boots hurt. The sunlight blinded him.

"Giddy-up!" said Slim.

"Giddy-up!" said Annie.

The horses galloped across the prairie, dust flying from their hooves.

"A-tchoo!" Jack sneezed as he bounced along into the setting sun.

6

Split the Wind

The sky was dark by the time they got
to the top of the hill. The wind was cool,
almost cold.

"Whoa," said Slim.

Dusty slowed to a halt.

"They're camped down there," Slim said in a low voice. "In that patch of trees."

Jack saw a campfire at the bottom of the slope. He saw the horses gathered in a dark clump. One let out a loud whinny.

"Hear that?" said Slim. "The mare. She senses Sunset is nearby."

The mare whinnied again.

"Seems like she's tied to a tree," said Slim. "I think the rest of the herd are loose."

"What's our plan?" whispered Jack.

"Smiley, you stay here and guard Sunset," said Slim.

"Right," said Annie.

"Shorty, you and I will ride down near their camp," said Slim. "You keep

Dusty quiet while I cut the mare loose."

How do you keep a horse quiet? wondered Jack.

"Once the mare's loose, she'll make for Sunset," said Slim. "Then you and Sunset set off, Smiley."

"OK," said Annie.

"Then we'll split the wind," said Slim.

What's that mean? thought Jack.

"Till we get to Blue Canyon," said Slim.

Where's that? wondered Jack.

"All set? Any questions?" asked Slim.

"No," said Annie cheerfully.

Yes – about a million, thought Jack.

"OK, pardners," said Slim. "See ya soon, Smiley. Come on, Shorty."

"Have fun," said Annie.

Fun? thought Jack. *Is she crazy? Our lives are at stake.*

Slim shook his reins. Dusty started down the slope. Their way was lit by a nearly full moon and a million stars.

Maybe now I can ask Slim some questions, thought Jack.

But just then voices came from the thieves' camp. They were nasty voices, followed by nasty laughter.

A chill went through Jack.

Dusty halted.

"This is far enough," whispered Slim. He slipped off Dusty.

"Keep him here," Slim whispered to Jack, "and keep him quiet."

"Wait . . ." whispered Jack. He needed more information.

But Slim was gone.

Jack gripped the reins and held his breath. He hoped Dusty wouldn't do anything.

For a moment Dusty was still. But then he snorted and started forward.

Oh, no! thought Jack. He tried to think of the rules on how to treat a horse.

He remembered: *a soft hand, a firm voice.*

He patted Dusty softly.

"Whoa!" he said firmly. To his surprise, Dusty stopped and was quiet.

Jack remembered another rule: *a sunny attitude.* He patted Dusty again. "Don't worry," he whispered. "Everything's going to be fine."

Just then a loud whinny came from the herd of mustangs. They began moving up the moonlit slope.

"Hey! The horses!" one of the thieves shouted.

A gun went off. Jack ducked.

"Come on, Shorty!" came Slim's voice. Jack looked up. Slim was riding the mare!

Jack was shocked. He thought that Slim was coming back to ride Dusty.

Instead, Slim rode right past him! As he got close to Annie, she set off on Sunset.

The mare galloped after Sunset. And the mustangs galloped after the mare.

Bang! Bang!

Jack shook the reins. "Come on, Dusty!" he said.

Dusty leaped after the mustangs. Jack nearly fell off. He clutched the reins in one hand and the pommel of the saddle in the other.

Bang! Bang!

The thieves were on their horses now. They were getting closer.

"Hurry!" Jack cried.

Dusty reached the top of the hill with an awkward leap. Jack started to slip out of the saddle. He let go of the reins and tried to hold onto the pommel, but his

weight pulled him down. He closed his
eyes as he fell to the ground.

Bang! Bang!

Oh, no, thought Jack, *this is the end.*

He opened his eyes. Dusty was
looking down at him. Jack scrambled up

and tried to climb back into the saddle.
It was hard without Slim's help.

As Jack struggled, he heard shouts from
the thieves. Their horses gave high-
pitched neighs.

Jack looked back.

A shimmering white figure was moving across the top of the hill. The thieves' horses were panicking and backing away.

Jack didn't have time to think about what he was seeing. He knew this might be his only chance to escape. Using all his strength, he pulled himself into the saddle.

"Come on, Dusty!" he shouted.

Dusty set off at full gallop over the prairie. Jack held on for dear life as they split the wind.

7

Ghost Story

Jack bounced in the saddle. He felt the cool night wind against his face.

He couldn't tell where they were going. But he trusted Dusty to follow the others.

Finally Dusty caught up with the herd as they began to slow down.

Jack shook his reins. Dusty came up beside Slim and Annie.

"Howdy!" said Slim.

"Howdy!" said Jack.

"Howdy!" said Annie. "Are you OK?"

Jack pushed his glasses into place. "Yes," he said. "You?"

"Yes," she said.

"That was some good riding, Shorty!" said Slim.

"Thanks," said Jack, smiling. He even liked being called "Shorty" now.

"Where are we heading, boss?" he asked Slim.

"Blue Canyon," said Slim. "OK with you?"

"Yes," said Jack.

"This way!" said Slim. He shook his reins and they all sped off again.

Slim steered the herd to the left. Soon he led them through a deep, narrow valley.

Finally they came to an open space surrounded by walls of rock and lit by moonlight.

"We'll keep the mustangs together here in Blue Canyon," Slim said.

He got off his horse. He helped Jack down. Annie slipped off Sunset.

"Take him to his mother," Slim told Annie.

Annie led Sunset to the mare. In the moonlight, the two mustangs touched noses and neighed.

As Jack patted Dusty's damp neck, he remembered the last two rules: *praise and reward*.

"Thanks," he whispered to Dusty. "You were great. You were really great."

Slim unsaddled Dusty, then handed Jack his saddlebags.

"Take these over to that grassy spot. We'll camp there," he said.

As Jack carried the saddlebags, his boots felt stiff and tight. His legs were sore and wobbly. But he didn't mind.

He threw down the saddlebags and his rucksack. Then he flopped down himself. He was very tired. Annie joined him.

"They seem so happy to be free and together again," she said, gazing at the moonlit mustangs.

"Yes," said Jack.

He lay back, using his rucksack as a pillow. He looked up at the stars.

"If we just had the answer to the riddle, everything would be perfect," he said.

"Yes," said Annie.

"Slim?" he called. "I have a question for you."

"What is it?" said Slim.

"Do you know the answer to this riddle?" Jack asked. "*Out of the blue, my lonely voice calls out to you. 'Who am I? Am I?'*"

Slim was silent for a moment, then said, "Sorry, Shorty, I don't know that one."

Jack's heart sank. "That's OK," he said. "We don't either."

"I have a question too," said Annie. "Why does the piano in the hotel play by itself?"

"I do know the answer to that one," said Slim.

"What is it?" said Annie.

"It's Lonesome Luke," said Slim. "He's the ghost of a cowboy who wanders the prairie."

Jack sat up. "I saw him!" he said. "I just remembered! He scared the thieves! If he hadn't come, I never would have got away!"

"Oh, yeah?" Slim chuckled. "Well, lucky for us, Lonesome Luke sometimes likes to help people out."

Slim threw his saddle down next to Jack and Annie and sat against it.

"Years ago, Lonesome Luke had a girl who he was just crazy about," said Slim. "She couldn't take the Wild West, though. So she went back east."

"What happened then?" asked Jack.

"Luke went mad. Every night he'd show up at the hotel and play the piano.

He played 'Red River Valley' over and over.

"Then one night he just vanished into the prairie and was never seen alive again. His bones were found a year later. But people say his ghost returns to the hotel piano to play 'Red River Valley'. It goes like this . . ."

Slim took out a harmonica. He began to play a song. It was the same sad song Jack and Annie had heard in the hotel.

Jack lay back down and listened to the lonely tune. A wild dog howled in the distance. The horses stirred in the dark.

I better take some notes, thought Jack.

But he didn't write a word before he fell asleep. He didn't even take off his boots.

8

Who Am I?

A fly buzzed past Jack's ear. He slapped it away. He opened his eyes.

The sun was high above the valley walls. He had slept for a long time.

Slim and Annie were sitting by a fire, drinking from twin mugs.

"Coffee? Biscuit?" Annie asked Jack.

"Where did you get them?" said Jack.

"A cowboy always carries biscuits and coffee," said Slim.

He walked over and gave Jack a biscuit and a mug of coffee.

"It's hard as a rock," Slim said. "And bitter as muddy river water. But a cowboy takes what he can get."

Jack took a bite and a sip.

The biscuit was very hard and the coffee was very bitter. But that was OK with Jack. Since cowboys didn't mind, he didn't mind, either.

"I'll saddle up Dusty," Slim said, "and take you back to town to catch your stagecoach."

"Then what will you do?" said Annie.

"Head south with my herd," said Slim. "Sell 'em. Then ride across the plains and round up more mustangs."

While Slim saddled Dusty, Jack took out his notebook and pencil. He wrote:

Cowboy breakfast
bitter coffee
hard biscuits

"Hey, Shorty," called Slim. "What are you doing?"

"Taking notes," said Jack.

"What for?"

"He likes writing things down," said Annie.

"Oh, yeah?" said Slim. "Me too. In fact, I first came out west to write a book. But one thing led to another. The next thing I know, I'm a mustang herder."

"Slim, you should write your book," said Annie. "And let the mustangs go free."

64

"Think so?" said Slim.

They looked at the grazing wild horses.

"I know so," said Annie.

"Yes,' said Jack. "Your book should be about the Wild West, Slim."

Slim kept staring at his herd. "Maybe you're right," he said. "I could settle in Laramie and write there. Wouldn't have to chase after horse thieves any more."

He turned back to Jack and Annie. "Yup, I think I'll be a writer. Let's go. Before I change my mind," he said.

"Yay!" said Annie. "I'll go and tell them." She jumped up and ran over to the mustangs.

Jack packed his rucksack, while Slim packed his saddlebags.

Then Slim and Jack climbed onto Dusty. They rode over to Annie, who was stroking Sunset's neck.

"I told him he's as free as the wind now," said Annie.

"Sounds good," said Slim. "Give me your hand, Smiley."

Slim pulled Annie onto Dusty. She sat in front of Jack.

Slim shook his reins. Dusty started off.

The sun was hot as Dusty climbed out of the valley. When they reached the top, they peered down behind them.

The mustangs pranced around playfully, their coats shining in the hazy light.

"They'll find their way out soon," Slim said. "Then head across the prairie. Shout goodbye to your pal, Smiley."

"Stay with your mother, Sunset!" shouted Annie. "Goodbye!"

Out of the blue, a voice called, "Bye!"

Annie gasped. "Who said that?" she asked. "The ghost?"

"Nope," said Slim. "It's just an echo. It's caused by sound bouncing off the rock walls."

He cupped his hands around his mouth. "Who am I?" he shouted.

"Am I?" came the distant voice.

"Oh, wow," Jack said softly. "That's the answer . . ."

"To Morgan's riddle!" said Annie.

"Echo!" she and Jack said together.

Jack looked at Slim. "You knew the answer last night," he said.

Slim just smiled and shook his reins. "Let's go, pardners," he said.

9
Lonesome Luke

The sun was low in the sky when they reached Rattlesnake Flats.

"Just leave us in front of the hotel," said Annie.

"You sure the stagecoach is coming through here?" said Slim.

"Yes," said Jack and Annie together.

In front of the hotel, Slim got down from Dusty. Then he helped Jack and Annie down.

"I hope you'll come to Laramie and visit me," said Slim. He winked. "I might be needing some help with my book."

"Of course," said Annie.

Slim climbed back on Dusty. He looked down at Jack.

"You know, Shorty," he said, "you might be short, but you're mighty tall in the brains."

"Thanks," said Jack.

"And, Smiley," Slim said, "your great courage is nothing to smile about."

"Thanks," said Annie.

"Good luck with your writing, Slim," said Jack.

"I'm grateful to you both for steering me straight," said Slim. "I promise I'll thank you someday."

"Really?" said Annie.

"A cowboy never goes back on his word," said Slim. Then he shook his reins, and Dusty set off down the street.

"Bye, Slim!" yelled Annie.

Slim Cooley turned round one last time. He waved his hat. "So long, pardners!" he called.

71

Then he rode off into the sunset.

Jack let out a deep sigh. "OK. I'm ready to take my boots off now," he said.

"Me too," said Annie.

They sat down on the veranda of the hotel. They started pulling off their boots.

"There!" Jack got them both off.

He wiggled his toes. He took his trainers out of his bag and put them on. Annie put hers on too.

"Wow – trainers have never felt so good," said Jack.

Suddenly the sound of a piano drifted through the air.

"Lonesome Luke!" said Annie.

Jack grabbed his bag. He and Annie crept across the veranda. They pushed open the swing door.

The piano was playing "Red River Valley". Sitting on the piano stool was the dim, shimmering shape of a cowboy.

Just then the ghost of Lonesome Luke looked at Jack and Annie. He waved a shimmering hand.

Jack and Annie waved back.

Then Lonesome Luke faded away. Cold air wafted past Jack and Annie. They both shivered.

"Let's go," breathed Jack.

They dashed up the dusty road. They ran across the cracked ground and past the graveyard. They ran until they reached the tree with the magic tree house in it.

Annie took hold of the rope ladder.

She hurried up and Jack followed. They were out of breath when they got inside the tree house.

Annie grabbed the ancient scroll. She unrolled it.

"Yay!" she said.

The scroll had one glowing word on it:

ECHO

"We got it right!" said Annie.

Jack picked up the Frog Valley book.

He pointed to a picture of the woods.

"I wish we could go there!" he said.

The wind started to blow.

The tree house started to spin.

It spun faster and faster.

Then everything was still.

Absolutely still.

10

Echo from the Past

Jack and Annie looked outside.

The sun had slipped behind the trees of the Frog Valley woods.

Annie still held the ancient scroll. She put it in the corner, next to the scroll from their ocean trip.

"Just two more to go," she whispered.

"Yes," said Jack. He unzipped his bag. He pulled out *Days of the Wild West*. He put it on top of a pile of books.

"Ready?" he said.

Annie was staring at the book. Her

mouth dropped open.

"What's wrong?" asked Jack.

Annie just kept staring.

"Have you gone mad?" said Jack.

Annie pointed at the Wild West book. "Read the cover," she said.

Jack picked up the book. He read the title aloud: "*Days of the Wild West.*" He looked at Annie. "So?"

"Keep reading," said Annie.

The author's name was below the title. It was in smaller letters. Jack read: *Slim Cooley.*

Jack gasped. His mouth dropped open. He and Annie stared at the words for a long moment.

"Oh, wow," whispered Jack.

"We were using Slim's book. The book he wrote after he left us!"

Jack and Annie shook their heads in wonder.

Jack opened Slim's book. He looked at the title page. At the bottom of the page, he read: *Texas Press, Dallas, 1895.*

Jack turned the page. He read the dedication:

WITH THANKS TO SMILEY AND
SHORTY, TWO STRANGERS WHO
CHANGED MY LIFE

Jack looked at Annie. "Slim dedicated his book to us," he said.

"Yes," said Annie. She smiled.

Jack put Slim's book back on the pile.

Then he and Annie left the tree house and climbed down the ladder.

As they started through the woods, the trees were alive with bird sounds. The air felt soft and moist.

"Frog Valley seems so peaceful," said Jack. "No rattlesnakes, no horse thieves, no ghosts."

"Yes, but no Slim Cooley either," said Annie sadly.

"I know," said Jack. "But when we read his book, it's like he's still talking to us."

"Oh," said Annie. "You mean it's like an echo from the past?"

"Yes," said Jack softly. "Wow."

Just then, out of the blue, a voice called, "Jack! Annie!"

"It's Dad!" said Annie.

"Coming!" she and Jack shouted.

Then they ran all the way home, through the long shadows of the setting sun.

Here are the words to
"Red River Valley",
the traditional cowboy song that
Lonesome Luke played on the piano.

From this valley they say you are going.
I shall miss your sweet face and bright smile.
For they say you are taking the sunshine
That has brightened my pathway a while.

Refrain (after each verse):

Come and sit by my side if you love me.
Do not hasten to bid me adieu.
For remember the Red River Valley
And the cowboy who loved you so true.

There never could be such a longing
In the heart of a poor cowboy's breast.
As dwells in this heart you are breaking
While I wait in my home in the West.

Do you think of this valley you're leaving,
Oh, how lonely and dreary it will be?
Do you think of the kind hearts you're grieving,
And the pain you are causing to me?

From this valley they say you are going.
I will miss your bright eyes and sweet smile.
For they say you are weary and tired
And must find a new range for a while.

Read on for a sneak peek
of Magic Tree House™ 11

LIONS ON THE LOOSE

1

Before Lunch

Jack and Annie were walking home from the supermarket. Jack's bag was heavy. It held a big jar of peanut butter and a loaf of bread.

"Are you going to have a peanut butter and jam sandwich?" said Annie. "Or a peanut butter and honey sandwich?"

Jack started to answer, but stopped.

"Oh, wow," he whispered.

"What is it?" said Annie.

"Look at *that*!" said Jack.

He pointed to the edge of the Frog Valley woods. In the shadows stood a small, delicate animal. It looked like a tiny deer.

"It's a sign," whispered Annie.

"Remember when we saw the rabbit? He was a sign of the Wild West."

The deer-like creature leaped into the woods.

Jack and Annie didn't stop to think. They followed as fast as they could. Jack's heavy bag thumped against his back as he ran.

Finally they stopped and looked around.

"Where has she gone?" Jack said.

"I can't see her," said Annie. "Oh, wow." She pointed up.

There was the magic tree house. It was shining in the afternoon sun, at the top of the tallest tree in the woods. Its rope ladder swayed in the shadows below.

"Where's Morgan?" said Annie.

Morgan le Fay wasn't waving at them

from the window. She wasn't even *at* the window.

"I don't know. Let's go up," said Jack.

They climbed the ladder and went into the tree house.

Sunlight streamed through the window. It lit a pile of books and two scrolls in the corner. The ancient scrolls held the answers to riddles Jack and Annie had solved earlier.

Jack took off his heavy bag.

"Has Morgan left us a third riddle?" asked Annie.

"Looking for someone?" said a soft voice.

Jack and Annie whirled round.

"Morgan!" said Annie.

Morgan le Fay had appeared out of nowhere. She looked ancient and lovely in the bright light.

"Do you still want to become Master Librarians?" she asked Jack and Annie. "So you can help me in my work?"

"Yes!" they said together.

"Wonderful," Morgan said. Then she reached into her robe and pulled out a scroll.

"You've solved two riddles so far," she said. "Here is your third." She handed the scroll to Annie. "And for your research . . ."

She pulled a book out from her robe and handed it to Jack. The book's cover said *The Plains Of Africa*.

"*Africa?*" said Jack. "Oh, wow, I've always wanted to go there."

He opened the book. He and Annie stared at a picture.

It showed hordes of zebras, tall giraffes, big animals with horns, and tiny, deer-like creatures.

"Hey, that's the animal that led us here!" said Annie.

"A Thomson's gazelle, I believe," Morgan said.

"Where are the lions?" said Jack.

"You'll find out," said Morgan.

"Um . . . maybe we need to plan this trip," said Jack.

Morgan smiled. "No. Go ahead. Make your wish now."

Annie pointed at the picture. "I wish we could go there," she said.

"Be careful," said Morgan. "Just keep an eye out."

"For what?" said Jack.

"The lions, of course," she said.

"Wait!" said Jack.

Too late.

The wind had started to blow. The tree

house had started to spin.

Jack squeezed his eyes shut.

The tree house spun faster and faster.

Then everything was still.

Absolutely still.